The Berenstain Bears®
Come Clean
for School

Nasty little germs

make you cough and wheeze.

Please cover your mouth

if you must sneeze.

Come Clean
for School

Jan & Mike Berenstain

HARPER FESTIVAL

An Imprint of HarperCollinsPublishers

Library of Congress catalog card number: 2010932912
ISBN 978-0-06-057395-9 (pbk.)
17 18   CWM   10 9 8 7 6
❖
First Edition

It was the first day back at school in Bear Country. Brother and Sister Bear were up bright and early. After washing up, they hurried downstairs to join Mama, Papa, and Honey Bear for breakfast. Papa was coming to school, too, as a parent helper.

Mama had bowls of hot oatmeal ready with "Have a Great Day!" written in raisins.

"Thanks, Mama!" said Sister, digging in to her oatmeal.

"Yum! Yum!" added Brother.

"Oh, boy!" said Papa. "I love raisins on my—ah-ahh-ahhh-CHOO!—oatmeal," Papa said, as he sneezed.

"Bless you!" said Mama. "But you should really cover your mouth and nose when you sneeze, Papa, so you won't spread germs."

ah-ahh-ahhh-CHOO!

"Germs?" said Papa. "Oh, piffle! Who's worried about a few germs among friends?"

Before Mama could say anything about Papa's views on germs, the cubs were grabbing their backpacks and heading out the door with Papa.

"Bye, Mama! Bye, Honey!" they called.

"Have a nice first day of school," said Mama. "Oh, wait—you should wash your hands. That's another way to keep germs from spreading."

"Wash our hands?" said Papa. "Oh, piffle! They look clean enough to me. Come along, cubs."

Mama sighed. The cubs always seemed to get sick at the start of school. But it was hard to get the family to follow good health rules.

I do hope they learn more about it in school, Mama thought.

At the bus stop, some cubs were coughing and sneezing. Most didn't bother to cover their mouths and noses. Sister gave her best friend, Lizzy Bruin, a big hug.

"Hiya, Lizzy!" said Sister. "Are you ready for school?"

"I doan feel berry good," said Lizzy, with a stuffy nose. "I thing I'm coming down wid a coad."

"Poor Lizzy!" said Sister. "You sound awful."

Papa shook hands with Lizzy's dad, who was also a parent helper for the day. But Mr. Bruin had a cold and kept blowing his nose. He sounded like a foghorn.

Soon the bus pulled up and they all climbed aboard.

When they got to school, they found there was going to be a special assembly. Dr. Gert Grizzly was giving a talk about good health rules.

"That should make Mama happy," said Papa. "You'll learn about all those nasty germs of hers."

Inside the auditorium, the school custodian, Grizzly Gus, was setting up a slide projector with Mr. Bruin.

"Hiya, Gus!" said Papa, shaking hands.

Grizzly Gus had a bad cough, but he didn't bother covering his mouth while he worked. Mr. Bruin kept blowing his nose.

The two of them made quite a racket. "Cough! Cough! HONK!"

Principal Honeycomb introduced Dr. Grizzly, and the slide show began.

"Hello, cubs!" she said. "You all know me. I'm the doctor who's been taking care of all of you since you were born. I see you when you are sick or hurt and I give you shots and medicine to keep you from getting sick. But today I want to tell you about something else that's important for good health—coming clean!

"Now let's talk about germs! They're too small to see except close-up through a microscope, like this. Germs are everywhere. They're in the earth, in the water, on things in your house, on your skin, and inside you. Some even float in the air. Most of them don't hurt you. But some of these little guys are big trouble.

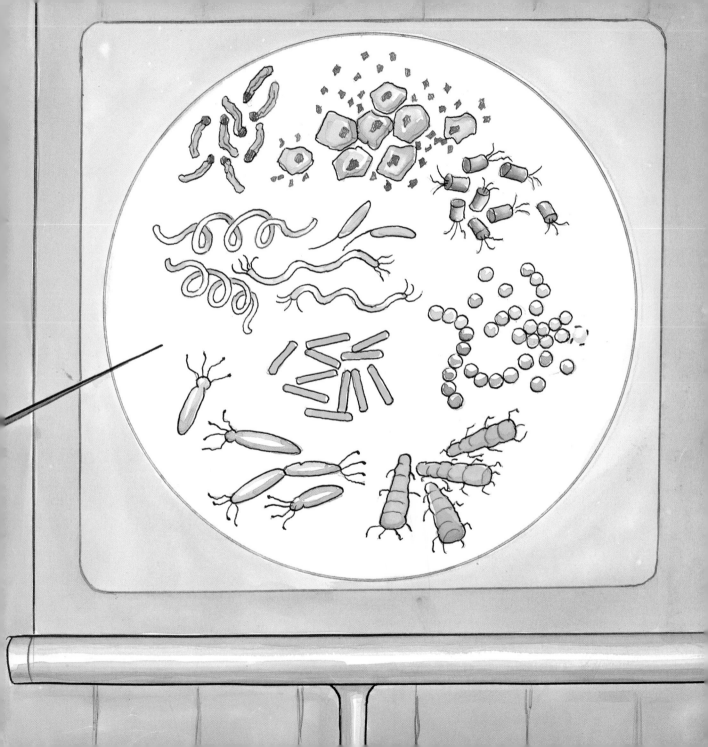

"This is the common cold germ. It's very, very tiny, but it can make you very, very sick. Some of you are coughing and sneezing. This little character is causing all the trouble.

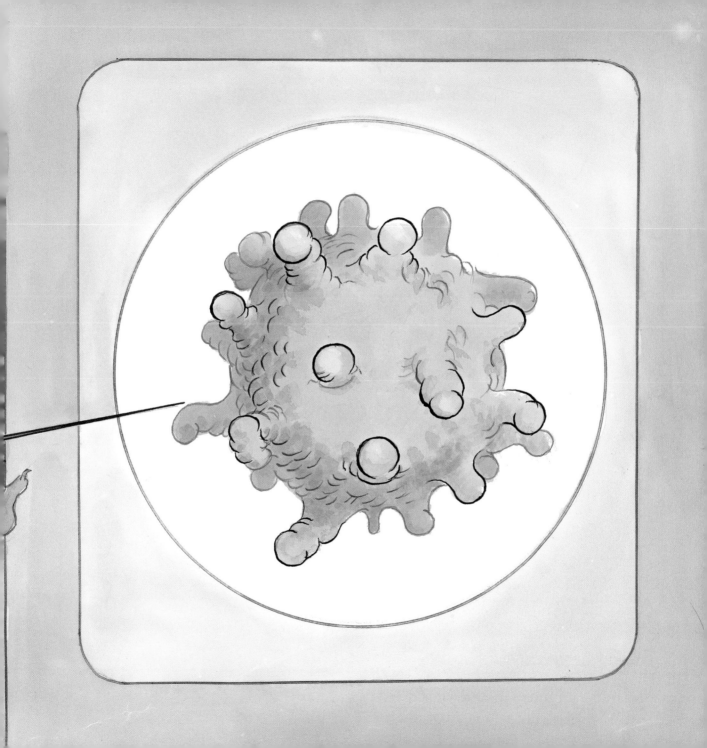

"What can we do about germs? We can start by making sure we don't spread them around. When we cough or sneeze, lots of germs get into the air. Then someone else may breathe them in and get sick. Always sneeze into your elbow and cover your mouth when you cough. That keeps germs from spreading.

"But the biggest germ spreaders are hands. Germs get on our hands, and we spread the germs by shaking hands or putting things in our mouths.

"To stop this, all you have to do is wash your hands. Washing with soap and hot water gets rid of germs. Always wash your hands before you eat and after you use the bathroom. In fact, it's a good idea to wash your hands whenever they are dirty. Try to wash for as long as it takes to sing 'Happy Birthday to You' twice.

"Now here's a friend of mine, Jerry the Germ, with a special message." The cubs all laughed and clapped and the slide show was over. "Now," said Principal Honeycomb, "I want to see all of you get off to a good start by going back to class and washing your hands."

The cubs were soon getting lathered up in the class art sink.

"Aren't you going to wash your hands, Papa?" asked Sister.

"Oh, piffle!" said Papa. "My hands are clean enough. I don't see what the big fuss is over a few little—ah-ahh-ahhh-CHOO!—germs."

"Bless you!" said Sister.

When the cubs got home from school that afternoon, they told Mama about what they had learned. Mama was very pleased.

"Isn't that wonderful!" she said. "That's just the message I've been trying to get across. What do you think, Papa?"

But Papa just sneezed. "Ah-ahh-ahhh-CHOO!"

"Bless you!" said Mama. "Are you all right?"

"I doan feel berry good." Papa sniffled. "I thing I'm coming down wid a coad."

Ah-ahh-ahhh-CHOO!

So Mama and the cubs put Papa to bed and gave him some nice hot soup. Then they all went and washed their hands!